Between Now
and Forever

Between Now and Forever

Lucinda Whitney

Lange House Press

Edited by Michele Paige Holmes
Cover design ©2020 Lange House Press
Layout and Formatting by LJP Creative
Published by Lange House Press

First Printing April 2020

ISBN-13: 978-1-944137-52-6

To Charlie,
the original dog.

CHAPTER ONE

*T*wo weeks at the beach.

Fourteen days of sand and sea and sunlight.

Time away from the library was just what she needed.

Sarah turned the key in the lock of the small house and pushed the door open. She grabbed her rolling suitcase and stepped inside, then paused.

Darkness enveloped the corners of the room and the air carried the fresh scent of a space recently cleaned. She flipped on the nearest switch and the small cabin she'd seen only in pictures lay before her—to the right side, one bedroom and a bathroom, and in front, a kitchen and living room dominated by a large window and sliding-glass doors leading to the back deck.

This late in the evening, the promised view didn't show much more than impending darkness with occasional twinkling dots, but that would change at first light.

Sarah closed the front door, walked to the glass doors and slid them open. The salty air in the night breeze instantly filled her lungs and the soft roar of the waves brought a smile to her lips.

Her shoulders relaxed in a long sigh, shedding the stress she usually wore as a constant mantle.

Rachel had been right—this was just what Sarah needed.

Sarah pulled out her phone and sent her best friend a message.

I'm here and it's amazing. Wish you could be here too.

Her phone rang and Rachel's name flashed on the small screen.

"I was beginning to worry," Rachel said. "Weren't you supposed to arrive an hour ago?"

"I got delayed at the airport and had to wait for a taxi." Plus, the driver had taken the wrong exit.

"In typical Sarah fashion," Rachel said. "That's why I'm usually the driver. But not this time."

"Not this time," Sarah echoed. "You have a more important job. How's Peanut? And how are you?"

"Peanut is doing great and so am I. Peter lets me get up only to go to the bathroom, so I guess I should be grateful for that. He's become a dedicated jailer."

"Peter loves you and wants what's best for you and the baby. Just hang in there. Before you know it, you'll be holding that beautiful little peanut of yours."

Sarah and Rachel had planned one, last best-friend's trip before the baby came, but complications to Rachel's pregnancy had forced her to bed rest. At first, Sarah had wanted to cancel their reservation, but after a lot of cajoling from Rachel and Peter, she'd come alone. It was a good decision. Not life-changing, but it would do her good.

"Easy for you to say. Just remember the pictures you promised me."

"Of course," Sarah agreed. "All the pictures we talked about."

While at St. Martin's Cove, she'd be taking photos of the small town and surrounding spots for a special photo book to be printed as a family keepsake and as a present for Peter.

"What about the cabin?"

"Conway Cabin is just like the pictures," Sarah replied. "A great little place."

"I guess you'll have to wait till morning for that walk on the surf."

"Not a chance. We planned a walk as the first thing we'd do and I'm taking that walk."

"In the dark?" Rachel asked.

"There's a waning moon outside. That's plenty of light."

"Just be careful."

"You too."

Sarah turned off the phone and breathed in deeply.

From the description on the website, the rental cabin stood within walking distance to the dunes on the beach, accessible from the backyard deck. The sound of the waves confirmed it.

She turned on the flashlight app on her phone and stepped down from the deck. The moon was out but didn't shine as brightly as she'd expected, and she stumbled a couple of times before finding the trail in the sand.

Once she got used to the terrain under her feet, she continued on and, as she approached the beach, the air stung sharper and the pull and crash of the waves raised in volume. In the low light, the swell of the dunes loomed on each side of the trail and beyond, and she could almost feel the wetness of the water. It was colder than she'd expected.

For a quick moment, the darkness overwhelmed her senses. Maybe this walk hadn't been such a good idea.

But she was almost there now. Just a few more yards and then she'd turn back to the cabin. She held the phone high and turned the light to shine in front of her, trying to gauge how far the water's edge was.

Her feet hit something first, then her knees buckled against an obstacle in the way.

"What the—" a male voice said.

Before she had time to react, she fell headfirst in a tangle of arms and legs and sand. Sarah screamed and a dog yelped.

For the longest instant, her world was upside down. Then a strong pair of hands grabbed her by the elbows and set her back on her feet.

"Are you okay?" a man asked.

In the darkness, alone with a stranger, her feelings reeled, and her heart thumped louder and faster as she tried to orient herself.

"My phone," she said, her voice still unsteady. She looked around and found the flashlight shining from the sand.

As she bent down to pick it up, the dog barked and she trembled. "Does he bite?" He was going to bite her and she had nowhere to run.

"No, he doesn't bite."

"He sounds like a beast."

The dog growled low as if he'd understood what she'd said, and she stepped back.

"Stay," the man said. At the simple command, the dog stopped growling and sat on his haunches beside his owner.

Panic surged within her. She was alone at night and away from any help. If the man or the dog attacked her, no one would come.

She teetered and he set his hands out as if to steady her.

"I'm okay, I'm okay," she said quickly. "I don't need help." Sarah palmed her phone and raised it up. "I'm going now."

He held his hands up in a gesture of surrender and took a step back. "Are you okay?" he repeated.

"I'm fine." She wasn't but she wouldn't tell him that. Her knee smarted and her forehead hurt something fierce. Most likely, a sizable goose egg was already forming.

"That was a nasty tumble you took." He slipped his hands in his pockets and kept his distance.

She still couldn't see his face clearly, but his voice was calm. Strangely, it calmed her down and her nerves receded as her heartbeat slowed. The dog remained in the same relaxed position.

"It wasn't my fault," she mumbled to herself. Not entirely. "I'm going now," she announced, walking backwards. "Don't follow me."

"Be careful. Don't go falling again."

After a few paces, she looked back over her shoulder. She couldn't see him clearly, but he stood on the same spot, the dog still at his side.

He raised a hand. "Have a good night, ma'am."

When Sarah passed through the back door, she managed to lock it before her legs gave out. She slid to the floor and leaned against the solid wood door, breathing hard and trying to make sense of what had just happened. The flashlight on the phone screen still shone brightly and she turned it off, then settled a hand over her chest.

What a crazy night. First, the taxi company had taken forever to find her reservation. Then, the driver had lost the exit, and taken even longer to arrive. And now, she'd tripped on a man and his dog on her way to the beach at night.

Well, he hadn't made the situation any better, sitting in the dark behind the dunes.

And to add insult to injury, he'd ma'amd her. How old did he think she was?

Not a promising beginning to a quiet vacation.

CHAPTER TWO

$\mathcal{D}$ean woke to the muted grayness of the early morning light through his window.

Another day of fog and humidity.

As the days shrank from fall into winter, fog would come to stay more and more. For today, it would most likely burn off as the sun pushed its way in. At least for the time being.

Charlie yawned and stretched on his rug on the floor, then stepped up to the bed with his tail wagging when Dean turned toward him.

"I know, I know," Dean said, running a hand across the dog's back. "We'll go for that walk. But first coffee for me and breakfast for you."

Dean padded to the kitchen and Charlie followed him, then the dog waited for his bowls to be filled with fresh water and food. While Charlie ate, Dean rinsed the coffee maker, got a new filter, and started a batch with his favorite dark roast.

He returned to the bedroom to put on his jogging clothes, his beanie, his zip jacket, and came back to the kitchen in time to fill a mug with the steaming coffee. Charlie waited patiently while he drank and a few minutes later, they set out together.

On their way down to the beach, Dean looked toward the small cabin, the closest house to his on this dead-end street. There were no other neighbors and he liked it this way.

That must be where the woman who'd tripped over him and Charlie was staying. He'd never seen the cabin rented out this late in the season. Why had she come to St. Martin's Cove in October? Didn't she know the weather would only turn colder with each passing day? And why had she been at the beach after dark? Some people were truly clueless. He could only hope she wouldn't be knocking at his door to borrow a cup of sugar as an excuse to chat.

After they jogged and walked for nearly an hour, all the way down to the cove, Dean set back with Charlie playing in the waves and chasing after the few seagulls on the surf.

To the east, the sun pushed on courageously, but it would be another hour before it burned through the fog.

A lone figure strolled in the opposite direction, a woman with shoulder length hair and a camera around her neck. Every so often, she stopped and took a picture of some object on the sand or raised the camera towards the sea.

Charlie barked and ran in her direction, but Dean called him back. She was most likely the renter and the last thing he needed was another encounter with an ill-humored woman.

But as their paths came closer to crossing, there was something familiar in her gait and manner.

Dean slowed down, then remembered the tennis ball in his pocket and threw it behind him for Charlie. He played with the dog for a few minutes and when he turned around, the woman was only a few yards away.

A woman he didn't think he'd ever see again.

And here she was. Right in front of him.

"As I live and breathe," he whispered. "Sarah Linden-Price."

Dean stared, his heart beating double-time, the ball forgotten, Charlie running circles around him.

She stopped. "Yes, that's me. Do I know you?"

The question lingered between them as she cocked her head with a slight frown between her blue eyes.

How he'd missed those eyes.

Dean grinned. "Yes, we know each other." He pulled off his wool beanie. "You probably don't recognize me with the beanie and the beard and the—"

"Dean Jensen," she said at last. "We had Ethics together. In my freshman year."

She remembered.

He slid his beanie onto his head and found it impossible to stop smiling. "I was a freshman too."

11

"I cannot believe it." She stared at him with a slight smile pulling at the corner of her lips. "It's been what, ten years?"

"Eleven," Dean replied. Eleven years and a few months since the last time he'd seen Sarah on his last day on campus.

She looked between him and Charlie and her expression fell. "That was you and your dog last night?"

He nodded. "That was us. How's your head?"

Was that a red bump near her hairline?

She covered her mouth with her hand. "I'm so sorry for the way I reacted."

"Don't worry about it. Let me introduce you to the beast. His name is Charlie."

At the sound of his name, Charlie flapped his tail enthusiastically.

Sarah swung the camera to her back, went down on one knee and extended her hand, then looked up to Dean for permission. "May I?"

"Yes, of course. He'll be your best friend."

She wrapped her hands around Charlie's neck and gave him a good scratching behind his ears. "Who's a good boy?" Sarah said in a sing-song voice. "I'm sorry I called you a beast. You're not a beast at all, are you? Such a good boy you are."

Charlie gave her the best version of his own grin, his tongue lolling out. He was in heaven, and so was Dean watching the exchange.

"Look at you," Dean said to Sarah. "You're a dog person."

"I am. I just never got around to getting one. What kind of breed is Charlie?"

"Just a mutt, I guess."

She stood and shook the sand off her knees. "Is he a rescue then?"

They set out walking with Charlie between them, who kept looking at Sarah with a decidedly loving expression. Dean couldn't blame him.

"Kind of. He was already living in the neighborhood when I bought the house. I'm sure he thinks of me as his rescue."

Sarah chuckled and the sound went straight to Dean's heart.

He'd missed her laugh as well, the way her eyes crinkled in the corners. She had a few more lines around them than before, but the authenticity was the same he remembered.

"How long have you been living in the area?" Sarah asked.

"It's going on five years." He didn't think much about it anymore, as he'd slowly become one of the locals.

"Quite the change from New York."

"Exactly," he agreed. "The pace here agrees with me."

"And what do you do?"

"I'm a freelance writer. But tell me, what brought you to St. Martin's?" he asked, eager to change the subject away from him. "I hope you didn't come expecting sunbathing weather."

13

"I had hoped for a bit more sun and a lot less fog, but I do know it's kind of late in the season." She bent down to pet Charlie, then continued. "I'm here to fulfill a project for a friend who was supposed to come and take pictures as a surprise for her husband. He spent his childhood summers with his grandparents who were from here, and she's making a photo book about it. Rachel was supposed to come but she's on bed rest under doctor's orders."

"You're still friends with Rachel?"

She frowned. "You remember Rachel?"

"Of course." He remembered everything about Sarah—the friends she had, the places she frequented, the books she read at the library on Saturday mornings.

But admitting to it would make him look like a stalker instead of the pathetically observant guy with a huge crush he'd been. So young and so pathetic.

Sarah nodded. "I forgot how popular Rachel was. It's been so long."

It hardly felt that long. The memories he'd tucked away had sprung back at the slightest nudge. In this case, the nudge was Sarah herself walking beside him at the beach in St. Martin's Cove, of all places. His nineteen-year-old self would have been ecstatic at the prospect of having Sarah beside him, conversing so easily. How many times had he imagined some version of this situation?

His present-day self was trying to make sense of the incredible reality.

Dean threw the tennis ball and Charlie bound after it with a happy bark.

Sure, Rachel had been the popular one, but she'd been too flirty for Dean's taste. Sarah had been the girl of his infatuation back then—her kind ways and soft words, her amazing blue eyes and how willing she'd been to discuss off-the-wall topics with him. He'd held on to every moment of interaction with her. She'd never known how he felt and he'd never told her.

Later, the regrets had come, wondering why he'd let the chance pass, knowing he would never know what might have been.

The experience had changed his perspective on life, and he'd gone from being less of a spectator and more to a participant—not waiting for things to happen, but going after them. Life was too short to wait.

And now here Sarah was.

Had life given him the second chance he'd wished for so long ago?

He glanced at Sarah who had quieted down and seemed momentarily lost in memories of her own.

Charlie galloped back and deposited the ball at Sarah's feet.

She chuckled. "You want to play?" She grabbed the ball and chucked it long, Charlie already on its trail.

"How easily he transfers his affections to you, the little traitor," Dean joked. "Not that I can blame him."

Sarah spared him a look, the curiosity evident in her eyes. "You've changed."

"I'm older and have more wrinkles," Dean replied.

"We both do," she agreed. "But there's something different about you. You used to be so shy."

He sobered. "I guess I grew out of it." In reality, he'd taught himself how to be more confident, as hard as that had been.

She transferred the camera to the front and picked it up. "Do you mind if I photograph Charlie?"

"Go ahead."

She knelt down on the sand and raised the camera to her eyes, clicking the shutter as Charlie ran back in their direction.

After a few minutes, they reached the path to her cabin and stopped.

Sarah turned to him. "It's been great to see you again, Dean."

It was great but not enough, and he wasn't ready to say goodbye.

"How long are you staying?" he quickly asked.

"Two weeks. Just long enough to visit and photograph all the places Rachel requested."

"How busy will that keep you?"

"It depends on the weather, but I'm hoping to have some free time."

"I hope you do." He held her gaze. "I'd like to see you again, Sarah Linden-Price."

The little smile tugged at her lips. "I'd like that, Dean Jensen."

"Good." Somehow, his voice kept calm. Inside, he was quite the opposite. "I'll see you later then."

"See you later, Dean. You too, Charlie," she added with a wave.

Sarah left toward the rented cabin and he stood watching until she unlocked the back door and went inside.

He definitely would see her later.

CHAPTER THREE

When the phone rang, Sarah turned off the faucet and propped the plate on the drying rack.

"You didn't call me last night," Rachel said when Sarah answered her call.

"I know. I'm sorry," Sarah said. "But you'll never believe what happened."

She told Rachel about her walk in the dark, the man, and the dog, and finding out the next morning they actually knew each other.

"Do you remember Dean Jensen from Ethics class?" Sarah asked.

"Dean Jensen?" Rachel asked. "The awkward guy? The one who always sat in the back?"

"Yes, that guy."

"He was cute but so shy," Rachel said.

"He's still super cute, but not shy anymore. And the years have been really good to him."

"How so?"

"He's broader and in really good shape," Sarah said, not even trying to hide the appreciation in her voice.

"You saw him without a shirt?"

"No, it's too cold for that, but he was jogging on the beach with his dog and wore the kind of clothes that showed him off to his best advantage, if you know what I mean."

"I do know what you mean."

"And he wears a neatly trimmed beard, kind of like a long weekend scruff, but well-maintained, and his dark hair has a natural curl to it—"

"You noticed all that, huh?" Rachel interrupted.

Sarah felt her cheeks warm. "I guess I did."

"In short, he's just your type, but if I remember correctly, you were partial to him back then too."

"I was?"

"You'd go on and on about his beautiful brown eyes at least once every other week after class."

Sarah suppressed a sigh. "He does have beautiful brown eyes. So expressive." Maybe she had noticed more about him than she wanted to admit to herself, let alone to Rachel.

"How much time did you spend with him?"

"We walked back together on the beach in the morning and took another walk in the afternoon. And his dog Charlie. Did I tell you about this dog, Rachel? Dean's dog is so adorable and loves to play with me. I took so many pictures of him."

"Yeah, you mentioned his dog." After a short pause, Rachel added, "Be careful, Sarah."

"What do you mean?"

"You're crushing on him already and you're only staying there for two weeks."

Sarah looked out the kitchen window and squeezed the edge of the counter. Was she crushing on Dean? Was that even possible in one day?

"There's nothing to worry about, Rachel. He's just being nice. That's all." She swallowed the lump in her throat. "I'll have to call you later. There might be a storm coming and I still need to go into town for some groceries."

"Have fun," Rachel said.

Sarah put on her jacket and cross-body bag, and locked the door behind her.

The owners had left the key to the lean-to shed on the north side of the cabin, which held assorted tools and two bicycles. She chose the bicycle with the basket and relocked the door, then set out on her way into town.

A wall of dark clouds loomed over the eastern horizon, but the storm wasn't expected until later in the afternoon, according to the weather app on her phone. She'd have plenty of time to go and return before then.

As she pedaled, Sarah thought of her conversation with Rachel. Her friend's words had taken her by surprise, especially the tone she'd used. Could Rachel be jealous because she was stuck at home? Or was Sarah too close to the situation to recognize the truth in Rachel's warning?

Neither made sense—it wasn't in Rachel's nature to be jealous, and Sarah wasn't the same young and naïve girl she'd been in college.

Twenty minutes later, she reached the outskirts of St. Martin's Cove. It was a small fishing town in northeastern Maine within shouting distance to its Canadian neighbors, as she'd heard Rachel repeat Peter's words about it. On the welcome sign, the town boasted a population of 2,957 and the best lobster in the state, which Sarah would have to put to the test.

Sarah rolled onto Main Street and quickly found the only market in town, St. Martin's Cove General Store. She locked the bike in the rack by the front, and went in. The name was apt, as the store was a mix of bakery, grocery, hardware supply, pharmacy, and a post office in the corner—everything a small town needed in one place. Effective.

A few people milled around the store, talking to the employees behind the various counters. Sarah toured the space, returned the greetings and smiles, and ended up in the bakery, lured in by the scent of freshly-baked baguettes. She added a few cans of soup to her shopping basket, a pound of apples, and Canadian butter to go with the bread.

By the time she placed her groceries in the bicycle basket, the storm hovered closer, much too close for comfort.

At the edge of town, Sarah felt the first splatters of rain, and ten minutes later she was drenched. She tried riding the bicycle but soon gave up, taking it by the handlebars and walking beside it. And if that wasn't enough, the bread was soaked, a sodden mess falling apart through the slats in the basket.

How long would it take her to walk home in these conditions?

Dejection slumped her posture and her chest squeezed with a heavy feeling, as if the rain weighed her down. The only option was to keep going.

A vehicle approached from behind and she turned to the shoulder, anxious to get away from the splashing rain. Not that it made much difference by now.

The driver honked the horn and she looked to find a pick-up truck. Instead of passing, the driver stopped right there on the side of the road, lights flashing and wipers moving swiftly, and a man exited.

"Sarah, what are you doing?"

Her shoulders sagged in relief at seeing Dean in a hooded rain slicker, a well-worn yellow one.

He didn't wait for her reply, but quickly opened the passenger door. "Get in," he said, taking her by the elbow with one hand and holding on to her bicycle with the other.

Once inside the warm truck, she leaned back and closed her eyes.

Dean returned a few moments later, and slipped the hood back from his head.

"My bike?" she asked, teeth shattering. "And the groceries?"

"All in the back." He reached behind her seat and tossed a blanket over her shoulders, then released the parking brake and resumed driving.

"Thank you," she managed.

"You're welcome," he said. "Why didn't you drive your car into town?"

"I don't have a car."

He glanced her way. "You didn't rent one?"

She shook her head.

"How did you get here then?"

"Flew in to Bangor. Took a train and a taxi the rest of the way."

He looked at her one more time, but didn't comment, probably judging her choices in transportation.

A few minutes later, they arrived at Conway Cabin. He parked in front of the cabin's picket fence. "If you give me the key, I'll open the door for you."

Sarah found the key in her bag and handed it to him. Dean pulled on his hood, ran ahead and unlocked the door, and she met him halfway on the path as he returned for her.

She opened her mouth to thank him when they reached the house, but he crossed the living-room to the fireplace. "This cabin is freezing," he said.

Sarah stood on the entry rug, still clutching the blanket around her, still wet and dripping on the floor. "The heater's not on?"

"It's a gas fireplace," Dean said, reaching inside the chimney. "I'm opening the flue so it vents properly."

"It's only the first week in October," she whined.

"This is St. Martin's," Dean said, turning a switch. "The weather is unpredictable this time of year." He shrugged. "Well, it's not much better in the spring either, but at least then it turns into summer."

Sarah watched him turn a series of small knobs while something clicked. "Are you sure there isn't central heating?" Why hadn't she read all the instructions for the cabin?

"There's a gas tank on the side of the house." He made adjustments and looked up at her. "I know what I'm doing, if you're worried."

"I trust you," Sarah said.

He stilled and stared at her, then cleared his throat. "You should go change out of those wet clothes and get in the shower to warm up. I'll fix you something hot."

Sarah turned to go, but then stopped. "Thank you, Dean. For everything."

His expression relaxed. "You're welcome, Sarah. It's my pleasure." He scrubbed the back of his neck and shook his head. "Not a pleasure that you were caught in the rain."

She nodded and held back a chuckle.

"I meant I'm happy to help you. Now please, go and take your time," he added.

Thirty minutes later, Sarah returned, dressed in her warmest lounge clothes and with her hair wrapped in a towel. A roaring fire burned behind the grate, and the living-room and kitchen had warmed considerably.

Dean stood in the kitchen. "Are you feeling better?"

"So much better." She gestured to the fireplace. "That fire feels amazing. Thank you."

"I'm glad and you're welcome." He carried a tray with mugs and bowls. "Come over. I got chamomile tea and chicken noodle soup."

He set the tray on the coffee table between the upholstered chair and they sat by the fire.

Sarah spied the thick slice of toast slathered with butter and picket it up. "Toast? Where did you get the bread?"

"I drove home to let Charlie out for his potty break and brought over an extra loaf of bread I had in the cupboard." He picked up his mug. "I wasn't able to save your baguettes, but the apples are in the fruit bowl on the counter and the butter is quite good. I've bought that kind before."

"Those baguettes didn't stand a chance against that deluge." She put down the nearly-eaten toast and stirred the soup. "Thank you so much for all this, Dean. And for picking me up from the side of the road when I looked like a drowned rat."

"I'd like to know how you plan to get around St. Martin's for your photo taking," Dean said. "If you don't mind my asking."

Sarah brought the cup to her lips and mumbled, "The bike."

"That's what I thought. Any chance I can convince you to rent a car?"

"You could convince me, but it wouldn't do me any good." At Dean's raised eyebrow, she added,

"I'm a genuine New Yorker and never learned how to drive."

"How did I not know that about you?" he asked, as if it were something important. "What about Rachel? Don't tell me she was planning to bike as well," he said.

"Not in her condition. She was the designated driver."

Sarah was used to adapting. As long as the weather cooperated, she would be fine riding the bicycle around St. Martin's Cove.

"Where did you get your rain slicker?" she asked Dean. "Do you think the general store might have one in my size?" She might as well prepare for the weather.

Dean shook his head with a low chuckle. "You're not getting a rain slicker, Sarah. I'll drive you where you need to go."

"What? No," Sarah said. "You will not."

He got up and took the tray with the empty dishes to the kitchen. "Yes, I will. I know the area anyways. It'll be more efficient. You still like being efficient, don't you?"

"Yes, I do." How did he remember that? She followed him. "What about your work?"

He filled the sink with warm water and soap. "I pretty much work for myself. My schedule is flexible."

Sarah stepped next to him. "Dean, I didn't come here for you to be my private driver. Or to have you wash my dishes."

He paused and turned to her. "Friends help friends. Will you let me be your friend?"

When he put it like that, and when he looked that way with those brown eyes of his all big and warm— how could she say no?

"At least, let me pay for the gas." She grabbed the sponge before he did.

He winked. "We'll see."

Why did she have a feeling he was only saying that to humor her?

CHAPTER FOUR

$\mathcal{D}$ean exited the truck and went around the front to open the passenger side door for Sarah.

After two days of colder temperatures and intermittent rain, today had dawned clear and sunny and almost warm. In the early afternoon, he'd driven Sarah to the western side of town, where she'd spent some time taking more photos for Rachel's project.

They returned a few hours later, and Dean took her to his favorite restaurant, looking forward to sharing a meal with her where they could sit across from each other and talk.

"What is this place?" Sarah asked.

"The best food in town," he said, as they went in.

"It's the only restaurant in town, isn't it?"

He glanced at her. "I guarantee you it's still the best. You'll remember this place when you go back to Manhattan."

Would she remember him too?

Sarah looked at the sign. "The Blue Crab?" She smiled. "Is that a dig at a certain seafood restaurant chain?"

Dean brought a finger to his lips and lowered his voice. "Shh. We don't speak that name here. Prepare to be amazed with the best Maine lobster boil of your life."

"The first one in my life too." She took a deep breath and looked around while they waited to be seated. "It smells amazing. I love how the tables are covered in butcher paper."

"It's quick and easy and leaves more time to concentrate on what's important."

"The seafood," she said.

"The seafood," he nodded.

A woman came over to lead them to a table. "Dean Jensen. 'Bout time you turned up."

"Sarah, this is Marianne Davis, one of the owners. Marianne, this is my friend Sarah, visiting from New York."

"Welcome, Sarah," Marianne said. "Aren't you in for a treat, if I say so myself. The boil?"

Dean nodded. "The lobster boil for two."

Some minutes later, a waitress came with a steamer basket and dumped everything on the table. "Enjoy," she said, leaving the tools for them to use.

Sarah's eyes widened. "My goodness, I don't know if I start with the lobster or the clams, or something else. It all looks so delicious and smells even better. Any tips from a seasoned local?"

"Adopted local," he corrected her then showed her the tools. "Use the cracker to break the shell and the fork to get the meat out. The rest, dig in. Get a plastic bib to protect your clothes, and there's paper towels and wipes."

"Dig in with my fingers?" She picked up a cracker and looked from him to the lobster in front of them. "This is going to be messy."

"It's part of the experience," Dean said. "Don't be shy. It's not the kind of meal to mind your manners."

She started slowly but soon took to it with enthusiasm. He loved how she didn't mind eating a potentially messy meal in public. A different kind of girl might have objected, but Sarah liked new experiences, and he loved that about her.

Dean watched her while they ate, and they talked about the locally-owned businesses in town. Every day they had spent together so far, he marveled at having her beside him—from their morning walks on the beach, to the afternoon drives to the places he knew and loved—for the little moments like this when he could take notice and drink her in and never tire of her company and presence.

The reality of spending time with Sarah Linden-Price was much better than all the daydreams he'd had in Ethics class eleven years ago.

"I always find the local history of a place and its people fascinating," Sarah said, as they discussed St. Martin's Cove. "When I take a vacation, I like to plan a new place with photography in mind. The landscape is different and the local customs are different, but, deep down, where it matters, people are the same. Many a time I end up at night with my nose buried in the family history of a place as I prepare for the trip."

"I felt the same way when I moved here. You should see all the books I have about local history and the families that settled St. Martin's."

"If that's an invitation, then I accept," she said breezily while wrestling with a lobster claw.

Dean paused momentarily from reaching for his next clam, the implication of Sarah's reply hitting him squarely. Quickly, he recovered, ate the clam, and added the same unworried tone to his reply. "I'll show you after dinner."

How was it that a thirty-year-old man could suffer the same kind of palpitations his nineteen-year-old self had endured? Traitorous heart.

When they arrived at his house, Dean unlocked the door and let Sarah in. "I can't vouch for the state of things. My roommate doesn't clean after himself."

She chuckled. "Excuses, excuses."

Charlie walked over to Sarah, tail wagging, and the biggest grin, and she obliged him with a warm greeting and a rubdown. "He's telling lies about you, isn't he, Charlie? I bet you're the best roommate."

As if in agreement, Charlie's tail wagged harder.

"Alright, alright. We've established my dog likes you better than he likes me. You don't have to rub it in."

Dean crossed the entry to the kitchen, turning only a few lights along the way, as Sarah followed him. By keeping the family room in the dark for now, her surprise would be greater when he turned the lights there. Hopefully, she would love it as much as he hoped she would.

"Let me open the back door to Charlie and then I'll give you the grand tour."

"Take your time."

Charlie didn't spend too long in the backyard, as if he couldn't bear to be separated from Sarah for too long. How peculiar that Dean could relate to his dog more than he could remember doing so in a long time.

"The house is from the early 1900s but I had it modernized," he said, then moved to turn on the lights in the eating area. "This is the dine-in kitchen. I don't entertain much, so I skipped on a dining room. There's a small pantry and laundry room this way, storage under the stairs, and a small bathroom just off to this side." He opened the doors as they went.

She nodded as she looked around. How did she see his place? What would she think of it and of him?

He continued to the front of the house, passing the staircase. "Upstairs, there's two guest bedrooms and a full bath. Through here, the master bedroom and private bathroom."

"Your bedroom?" Sarah asked.

He nodded, pushing the door ajar. At least, he'd made the bed this morning. Kind of. Not his best job. His weight-lifting equipment remained on the floor where he'd left it instead of being neatly tucked away.

"Do you ever miss the city?"

"Not really." Not one bit. "St. Martin's Cove suits me and I like it here. It's peaceful and quiet which is perfect for my work."

"You don't see yourself moving back at all?" she insisted.

"I won't say never, but it would have to be for a very strong reason." He still owned the apartment in Manhattan, at the recommendation of his financial adviser, but hadn't been there in a long time.

"You're saving the best for last," she said, as he led her back to the other side of the house.

Dean looked over his shoulder at her and gave her a little smirk. "Am I?" He stopped and turned on all the light switches to the great room and library, one at a time.

Sarah gasped. "Oh, floor to ceiling shelves. And a large window flanked by window seats. This is the home library of my dreams."

Her declaration warmed his heart. He should have known she would be impressed, as she'd mentioned she worked as an acquisitions librarian in Manhattan.

Dean watched her as Sarah took to the room with a large smile on her face.

The library wall spanned the width of the house, interrupted by the fireplace and a large sofa in front of it, with the reading corner to the front and his desk facing the picture window with the view of the beach.

As Sarah approached the shelves, Dean walked over to the desk, making sure his laptop computer had the screen turned down.

She glanced at him. "And now I'll discover your secrets by looking at the books you read."

She just might, and he wasn't prepared for that. Not yet.

To keep himself busy while she perused his shelves, Dean moved to build a fire.

"I see an attempted organization here," she said. "These shelves are fiction, mostly by alphabetical order and genre. Could I interest you in the Dewey Decimal System? It's really quite simple."

He looked over his shoulder. "Only a librarian would say that. Are you caressing the spines, Sarah?" he asked.

"Definitely." As she went, she commented on whether she owned a book, had read another book, or wouldn't be caught reading a certain book, her voice raising and lowering according to her interest. Sometimes she added which section the book would be in the library where she worked, and how popular it was with readers. Dean added his own opinion to hers and they teased each other about some of their choices and preferences.

"You have the Symbols & Secrets series. I've read this one."

Dean froze. "Yes?" He tried to ascertain her tone—was it positive or negative?

"Everett Ward is an amazing character," she said,

holding the first book in her hands and leafing through it.

Relieved, he continued poking the logs in the grate. "He can be."

"But, of course, the true hero of the series is Theodora Callahan," she continued. "Michael D. Williams should give Thea a bigger role than secretary-slash-sidekick to Professor Ward."

"I'm not surprised you think that way," Dean said with genuine interest. He'd love to talk about his characters with Sarah and see what suggestions she had. It would prove to be an enlightening discussion, he was sure of that.

"It's a popular series," she added. "I've had to purchase many copies as the books are constantly requested by patrons. One time, I emailed the publisher, Sunrise Press."

Dean sat up. "That author's publisher?"

She nodded. "The events coordinator had already sent an email asking for an appearance by Michael D. Williams without much success, so she asked me to send another request. I did, but the reply was the same as the one she'd received—the author values his privacy and doesn't participate in public events."

It was true. His lawyer had been able to get that clause in the contract, at the expense of a percentage of the royalties. Dean had never wished to make an exception, but, if he ever told Sarah he was the author, he might consider it. What would she say if he told her right now?

"Maybe it was for the best. Sometimes, the really famous authors can be such divas, you know? The stories I could tell you," she said with a conspiratorial tone and a slight eye roll.

"I can imagine," he replied. He'd heard that said about him before, about being a first-class snob who didn't care about his readers. It shouldn't surprise him but it wounded his pride to see Sarah saying something similar. No one else was to blame for it but himself.

"How do you have book four already? Doesn't it come out in a couple of months?"

He scrambled for a reply. "From the publisher." That much was true. "For an editorial." But this wasn't.

"Advanced copies are a good perk of my job as well, but I haven't received this one yet." She moved on to the next shelf and he breathed out a little easier.

"This little book," she said, pulling a small volume from the shelf. "This was one of my favorites in freshman year."

"Which one?"

"*The Science of Simple Hugs: Reflections for Long Days in the City.*" She held up the spine.

"I remember." He'd bought it and ready it after watching her carry it for weeks on end.

"I thought it made me look mysterious and interesting, but I was just the biggest book nerd."

"Watch it, missy," he said in a mock stern voice. "Book nerds are the best kind of people. And I got the book because I found you interesting and mysterious." He'd been intrigued by the title and the girl carrying the book.

She glanced at him sideways with a raised brow and returned the book to its spot. "What about the companion book?"

"There's another one?"

"Yes, *The Art of Kissing in the Rain: Musings for Friday Nights at Home*. It came some years later and I loved it just as much."

"I didn't know there was a second book," he admitted. The title sounded as compelling as the first one's, and they gave him all sorts of ideas—hugs and kisses.

"Biographies, non-fiction, reference," she itemized, oblivious to his rampant thoughts. "What did you study in college? I don't remember if it ever came up."

"A major in history and a minor in political science." With interests in sociology and environmental psychology, among other things, which depended on the research he needed for whatever the work in progress was.

"Hence the large history section." She turned to him. "Have I read anything you've written?"

He shrugged. "You might have." As much as he loved her curiosity and interest, he wasn't ready to let her know what he really wrote. "Here's the section about St. Martin's Cove history," he hurried on to say, showing her to the shelves.

Maybe the distraction would lead her to ask different questions, ones that didn't threaten his secret identity.

He would tell her as soon as the right moment came along.

CHAPTER FIVE

A persistent ringing reached Sarah's conscious-ness as she lay in bed. She raised her head to look at the digital alarm clock on the bedside table. It read five thirty in the morning. Too early to get up.

A few moments later, the ringing returned. This time, Sarah was half awake and more aware than before. She palmed her phone and accepted the call when she saw Dean's name flashing on the screen.

"It's an ungodly hour, Dean Jensen," she mumbled. "You better have a good excuse."

"Good morning, Sarah," he replied too brightly. "I'm guessing you forgot about our early morning outing."

She groaned. "Is that today?"

He chuckled. "Dress warmly. I'm picking you up in fifteen minutes."

After hanging up, she turned in bed and stared at the phone. Something nagged at the back of her mind, something she'd been thinking about before going to bed. Then she remembered—the book. She wrote herself a note to ask Rachel and Peter for help since it was too early to wake them up.

Reluctantly, Sarah dragged herself out of bed and dressed in as many layers as she'd brought with her.

In the few days since her arrival at St. Martin's Cove, she had established a new routine.

In the mornings, she called Rachel while having breakfast, and told her of what she'd done the day before, where she'd gone and what she'd photographed, usually minimizing how much time she'd truly spent with Dean.

After the phone call, Sarah uploaded the photos from the day before, did some light editing, and worked on the book layout, and some other projects she had on her computer, until the early afternoon.

Somehow, she and Dean spent most of their afternoons together, what with him driving her around and serving as her guide to all things local. On some occasions, their time would stretch into the evenings as well, either at her rental cabin or his home, in which case he and Charlie returned Sarah to her front door until she was safely inside.

It was easier to keep the detailed account from Rachel, concentrating only on the activities and places Sarah knew her friend expected. They had planned the itinerary together after all.

Then why did Sarah feel like she was a teenager going behind her parents' backs to see the boy they had reservations about?

The situation was different, but the feeling was nearly the same—a pinch of guilt, some regret, and a large dose of excitement. She would be lying to herself to say she didn't enjoy Dean's friendship. He was the ideal companion on her trips, considerate and funny, and he seemed delighted in doing things for her, in surprising her with something he knew she needed or liked.

How could she not bask in the attention of an attractive man who enjoyed her company?

By the time Dean knocked on her door, Sarah was ready. She grabbed her camera bag and her knit hat, and met him with a yawn.

"The sun's not up yet," she said, maybe a little crankier than she meant.

He opened the passenger side door for her. "Yes, that's the point of leaving at this time."

As Dean drove off toward the south, Sarah kept yawning.

He glanced at her. "Now I'm feeling guilty for dragging you out so early, but I promise it'll be worth leaving your bed."

"I'm sure the bracing cold will wake me up."

"What about a nice warm Mainer breakfast afterward? There's a great place in the next town and it's not too far."

"You should have led with that," she said. "That's the kind of incentive to get out of bed for."

Dean grinned. "I'll keep that in mind for future reference."

It wasn't the first time Dean alluded to the future, implying they would spend time together again. Did he mean while she was here at St. Martin's Cove or beyond her visit? And if he meant the latter, how would that even work with him here and her in Manhattan?

Sarah didn't want to entertain anything beyond the here and now—the future was complicated, and it involved too much thinking. For the time being, spending each day with Dean was the kind of simplicity she needed, without having to worry about what she couldn't change. That would come later, if it came at all.

"There it is," Dean said, interrupting her thoughts.

Ahead of them, at the farthest tip of the cove, stood a lighthouse with a white-washed tower and a black cupola. Sarah took a breath, already planning the photos she would take.

He pulled to the side of the road and parked, then got out and walked to the back of the truck where he retrieved a burlap sack and some tools.

"Are we not getting any closer?" Sarah asked as she followed him.

"We are, but this is the best place for you." He checked the time on his phone. "Sunrise will be in a few minutes and you won't want to miss it."

The framing for photographing the lighthouse was perfect from the spot in front of the truck. Sarah looped her camera around her neck and set up the unipod stand. "You're right. This is the best spot."

He nodded with a smile. "Good. I'll be out of your way. Just send me a text if I'm too far out to hear you."

"What will you be doing?"

He raised the tools and sack. "I'll be clamming. It's low tide."

As Dean walked off in the direction of the beach, she called out to him. "Thank you!"

He turned and waved.

A small smile tugged at the corners of her mouth. The man was unexpected. Every time she thought she had him figured out, he said or did something that surprised her. He was the opposite of the few guys she'd dated before—the metro, intellectual type—but more and more her attraction to him grew, and she didn't want to stop it from developing.

She turned her attention to the scene before her. As the sunrise inched its way above the sea, the colors glided across the water and sky, timidly at first, then coming in a wave of tones and light.

Were all the sunrises this beautiful or was nature putting on a special show for her?

These moments alone, just her and the camera capturing the amazing sunrise and lighthouse, were a gift. A thoughtful gift from Dean. He'd known she would love it and she did.

Sarah panned the landscape for a wider shot and caught sight of Dean on the long stretch of wet sand the low tide had exposed. She zoomed in and composed a new frame to take a picture of him, a lone man working by himself, a silhouette against the early morning colors.

After she spent all the time she wanted photographing the cove and the lighthouse, Sarah went to the beach. She met Dean already on his way back, carrying the sack in one hand and the tools in the other.

She lifted the camera and took another picture of him, with the beach and the water and the sun providing the background. He made a perfect subject, with his rugged good looks and his crooked half-smile warming up his eyes.

He shook his head good-naturedly and, once closer, said, "What was that for?"

Sarah flexed a pose pretending to be him. "Behold, the mighty hunter. Or, in this case, the mighty fisherman."

"Clammer," Dean corrected, his tone amused. "The person who goes clamming is a clammer."

"That doesn't sound half as mighty."

He chuckled. "I suppose not. But I did get treasure."

He held up the sack and Sarah peeked inside to find it about a third-full of clams.

"You got some nice big ones. How does clamming work?"

They made their way back to the truck. "Pretty much like fishing. I bought a yearly license and I can get only what's allowed by law, a little under half of a five-gallon bucket, and the bigger ones in size."

Once at the truck, Dean laid the tools at the back. He reached for a portable cooler and deposited the sack with the clams inside. "There's a bag of ice at the bottom with a thick layer of newspaper on top. You don't want the clams in direct contact with the ice."

"Tonight's dinner?" she asked.

"For tomorrow. They need to purge the sand and impurities and be cleaned." He secured the cooler and closed the tailgate. "What does your calendar look like for tomorrow night?"

They went around each way and entered the cab.

"Are you asking if I'm available for a homemade dinner with the clams you caught yourself?"

"Particularly specific and accurate," he said with a raised brow and a smirk. "A homemade meal by yours-truly and, if that's not enough to entice you, an after-dinner surprise. Plus, Charlie will be there."

Sarah looked at him and rubbed her temple. "After-dinner surprise?" Was he suggesting something?

His expression fell and he glanced at her. "That didn't come out right." He hurried on to say, "I'm sorry. That's not what I meant."

Dean winced and looked away for a moment, and Sarah found his embarrassment endearing.

"That's good to know," she assured him. "Just checking."

"I have a telescope set up in one of the attic bedrooms."

"There goes the surprise." She chuckled.

"Yeah, there goes the surprise. But at least, you don't think I'm propositioning you." He paused and blushed. "Not that I wouldn't want to—I mean, I would—" he sighed deeply. "I better stop talking," he said at last. "Let's have that breakfast."

"Sounds like a good plan." She covered her mouth to disguise a smile.

"With food in my mouth, I won't be able to talk."

This time, she laughed.

CHAPTER SIX

𝒟ean's time with Sarah was running out.

She'd been in St. Martin's Cove for eight days already, and would be leaving in a week. What had started with her being caught in the storm on a bicycle and him offering to drive her around had continued every day since then. In the beginning, they had met in the afternoon, but soon the outings had expanded to include early morning or evening, and often both. Tonight he planned to show her the night sky through the roof skylight window in the eastern attic bedroom. He had a feeling Sarah would enjoy stargazing.

Today had been different and they hadn't spent time together yet. Since the weather had been sunny and much warmer in the past few days, Sarah insisted on taking her bike into town for some shots of Main Street and the public buildings. He'd taken the time to return his editor's call and give him an update on his project, which turned into a longer conversation than he'd planned for. Then he'd cleaned the house, made sure the telescope was ready to be set up, and drove to the general store to pick up a few of the ingredients he needed for tonight. Once back at the house, he'd started on preparations for dinner.

A knock sounded at the door. Dean glanced at the digital clock on the stove and frowned. He wasn't expecting anyone other than Sarah and he would be picking her up in thirty minutes so she didn't have to walk alone.

He opened the door and found her there. "Sarah." The anticipation to see her had simmered all day, and now she was here. "Charlie and I were coming to get you."

At his name, Charlie made a hasty appearance.

She followed after them and closed the door behind her. "I know. I'm sorry but I couldn't wait around doing nothing."

A bloom of hope danced in his chest. Did that mean she couldn't wait to see him as well?

Dean glanced over his shoulder, unable to keep the smile from his face. "Don't apologize. I'm glad you came earlier." It meant more time with her, and he would never say no to that.

She placed a glass bottle with a swing top on the counter. "Freshly squeezed lemonade. I didn't know what else to contribute, but something to drink is always suitable, right?"

"Absolutely. Even though you didn't have to bring anything but yourself." He took the bottle and stuck it in the refrigerator.

Sarah inhaled deeply. "What smells so good in here?"

"That would be the blueberries for dessert." The oven timer went off and he approached to press it. "I'm roasting these in intervals of four minutes and they need another shake." He grabbed a pot holder, opened the oven, removed the baking sheet, and gave it a good shake. Then put it back in and set the timer again. "One more shake they'll be done."

"Roasted blueberries for dessert. Are you trying to impress me?" she asked with a teasing smile.

She had no idea how much. "You hadn't noticed yet?" He sent a quick little wink her way, liking the flirty banter between them.

Was it too early to make a move beyond friendship? To let her know he was interested in something more? What if she didn't feel the same way? What did he have to lose?

Her friendship, for starters.

This was the reason why he hadn't dated in years—the difficulty in knowing which decision to take was much too real at times. Living the single life was simpler but also much lonelier, and Sarah's presence in his life for the past week had brought that difference more sharply into focus. He was ready for something more.

Dean put the distracting thoughts away and concentrated on Sarah instead. "Are you hungry? Should I get started on dinner?"

"I'm starved," she said, coming into the kitchen. "I had an early lunch in town but that was hours ago. What can I do to help?"

He opened the refrigerator and removed the colander full of clams, the fresh herbs, and the butter, and put them all on the counter. "Would you like to chop the parsley and chives?"

"Are you trusting me with a knife?"

He frowned at her. "Should I not?"

"I'd feel more comfortable with a pair of scissors."

"Where's your sense of adventure, Sarah?" he teased her.

She raised an eyebrow. "Don't say I didn't warn you."

Dean retrieved the cutting board, the chef knife, and a small glass bowl, and handed them to her.

Sarah took the spot to the left of the sink and quickly set up a station. "Don't expect an even chop."

"As long as you keep your fingers out of the way, you'll do fine."

He removed the blueberries from the oven and put them aside for later. To take advantage of the remaining warmth inside, he put a couple of baguettes on the middle rack.

They worked side by side as he cooked the simple meal. He chopped a small onion and sweat it in butter and olive oil on a skillet, then added minced garlic and, a few minutes later, some white wine. After adding the clams, he put the lid on the skillet and waited for the clams to finish cooking.

Sarah had already set the table and sliced the bread, and Dean retrieved the lemonade from the refrigerator. She took a seat and Charlie settled on the floor by her feet.

"Not much longer now," he said, again at the stove, as he added the chopped herbs to the sauce before turning off the burner.

"When did you become so proficient in the culinary arts?" Sarah asked.

"I'll tell you a little secret. Steamed clams just look fancy, but they're super easy to make."

"It looks super fancy from here."

"You know how the single life is, cooking for one. There aren't any options for delivery out here and the Blue Crab is the only restaurant in the area. I could go to the next town, but I get lazy."

"So it's less lazy to learn how to cook?" she asked.

He shrugged, and Sarah chuckled.

He loved this easiness between them, to see her so relaxed and at home in his space. He continued, "I usually cook simple meals with few ingredients. Nothing too difficult."

He gave the pan a last swirl and removed the lid, then carried the skillet to the table. "Here we go," he said, placing the skillet on a trivet. "Steamed clams in a garlic-parsley-chives butter sauce."

"They smell amazing, Dean."

He ladled a good portion into her soup plate. "Wait until you try them. This is my favorite way to eat clams."

"Is the bread for the sauce?" Sarah asked.

"Yes, to mop it up." He served himself and they spent the next few minutes eating, with Sarah declaring these were the best clams she'd ever had.

Dean took the compliments with appropriate modesty, insisting it was an easy recipe, but inside, his heart swelled in easy happiness to have her there with him.

Afterward, he cleared the table and brought over the roasted blueberries in a serving bowl, followed by the glass jars filled to three-quarters with the cheese mousse he'd prepared earlier.

"Ooh, what's this?" Sarah asked in a curious tone.

"A simple dessert to highlight the state fruit of Maine," Dean told her. He placed the small glass container in front of her along with a spoon, and repeated the same for himself. "Now the roasted blueberries go on top."

Sarah followed his instructions and took a spoonful, and Dean did the same, waiting for her reaction.

After a moment, she removed the spoon from her mouth, but continued to lick it. "Did you come up with this recipe?"

"Do you like it?"

"I love it," she replied, taking another bite.

Dean grinned. "The original recipe called for goat cheese, but I couldn't find any, so I substituted some mascarpone and plain yogurt, which were whisked with heavy whipping cream and some sugar." He ate a spoonful of his own. "I think it turned out pretty well."

"It's simply divine. The texture of the blueberries, so much like a jam, and the smoothness of the cream, or mousse, with a bit of tangy at the end." She made an appreciative sound. "I think it's my favorite dessert ever."

"That's a high compliment. I'll send the other two jars home with you."

"I should say no, but I won't. I'll take an extra walk at the beach instead." She raised her spoon in a salute. "It'll be worth it."

"Do you want the recipe?"

"I might, even though the cooking talent passed me over completely. As for yours, it's not being fully appreciated."

"How so?"

"You don't have anyone to cook for and enjoy your creations," she said, as if stating the obvious.

"I'm cooking for you." He would cook for her many more times, given the chance.

"That's not what I mean, and you know it," she insisted. At his own, raised eyebrow, she continued, "How come you're not married and cooking for your wife and family?"

He put his spoon down and leaned back, trying to gauge her attitude. "Are we talking about past relationships right now?"

"Why not? We've pretty much talked about every-thing else."

She was right, of course. The past few days had afforded them the time and occasion to talk about as many topics as they could come up with. But they'd held back as well, evading anything too personal. Like the pain of lost loves.

He adjusted his chair. How much did he want to tell her? Somehow, he wasn't ready to share every-thing, but he didn't want to lie to Sarah. "I had a girlfriend when I lived in the city. We dated a while and I thought we were getting serious. I hadn't pro-posed, but we'd talked about marriage."

He paused and Sarah asked, "What happened?"

"My career took a change." Dean cleared this throat. "It came with a raise."

"So you had more money," she said.

"Yeah, you can say that." His career had actu-ally taken off at the speed of a bullet train and the money soon followed. "I told Lisa and she was very happy for me. At first, I didn't see the shift in her attitude, but gradually she started buying things and asking me for money to pay for them. It got to the point where she took my credit card and when I confronted her about it, she didn't think it was a big deal." He shrugged. "According to her, I had the money, so why couldn't she use it?"

Sarah stared at him for a moment. "That's—I don't even know what to say."

He nodded. "She broke up with me and I moved here."

"She broke up with you," Sarah repeated.

He nodded, the mood suddenly more sober than he'd intended.

"I can see why you think it's safer to cook for one."

Dean appreciated her not pushing for more details. "What about you? Do you cook for one?"

"Not if I can help it." She chuckled. "I get take-out, meal delivery services, or a bowl of cold cereal when I forget to plan something."

"In my expert opinion, I think you would like having someone to cook for you," he said lightly.

"I'm sure I would. Rachel did when we were roommates. She cooked and I cleaned, but then she got married. As for ex-boyfriends," she paused and sobered before going on. "The one serious relationship I had was a while ago and I haven't really dated since then."

"You don't have to tell me if you don't want to," he said.

"I don't mind. Carl and I met in my junior year. He was a fun guy and that was attractive to me in the beginning. We went out a lot and were together for quite some time and just about when I thought we were getting more serious, he got a promotion that involved moving to Colorado and he didn't tell me any of it. I happened to see a piece of mail at his apartment one day—a rental contract for a place in Denver. I'd had no idea he was moving, and asked when he'd been planning to tell me. He shrugged and said he hadn't really considered it important, as we'd always been fun, not serious."

"He sounds like one of those guys who definitely needed to grow up," Dean replied. A dumb guy who didn't know what a treasure Sarah was. In a way, his and Sarah's experiences were not so different. "I'm sorry." It sounded trite.

"It's okay," she said a bit too brightly, then stood and took the dessert jars to the sink. "Where's that telescope you promised?"

"Right this way," he said, leading her to the stairs.

He hadn't thought about Lisa in a long time. The situation with her had been a wake-up call for him. Losing trust like that had been hard and he hadn't been willing to go through something similar again.

Until Sarah came back in his life.

CHAPTER SEVEN

$\mathscr{S}$arah followed Dean up the staircase to the raised attic, glad for a few minutes to think through what he'd told her.

He had trust issues and she couldn't blame him after the way his ex-girlfriend had treated him. From what Sarah had seen, his house was comfortable and without any opulence or excess of any type, which meant he wasn't flouting his fortune, however large it might be. It was somewhat confusing, to think he might have the kind of money that had caused his ex to deceive him.

As for Sarah, she didn't trust men easily either, not after Carl had moved on from her life so abruptly, as if she'd been nothing more than a pal to hang around with. What was it with the guys who only wanted the fun life? What about commitment and sharing a life completely? And what about falling in love?

"It's in the eastern bedroom," Dean said, interrupting her thoughts.

She brought herself back to the present, paying attention to what he said and the new surroundings.

There was a bathroom at the top of the stairs and a short hallway leading to the sides in both directions. She followed him to the right and entered a sparsely furnished bedroom with a large window on the ceiling.

"I haven't seen a window like that before," she said, entering the bedroom.

Dean had gone ahead of her and scooted the floor telescope out of the way, then pushed a handle. "It's a roof skylight window and it opens up and forward to allow more access." As he demonstrated, the pane above him formed a covering parallel to the floor and another pane straightened out ahead to create a sort of small balcony.

"Would you switch off the ceiling light, please?" he asked her. "Leave the one in the hallway on but close the door a little."

She did as he asked and walked back carefully, letting her eyes get used to the semi-darkness.

He motioned her closer and Sarah approached the open window to a view of the night sky stretched unfettered ahead of them.

"It's a new moon tonight," he said, standing closer than she'd believed him to be. "Perfect for star gazing."

Overlooking the beach and the sea beyond, the darkness provided the ideal backdrop without too much light pollution. She trembled and folded her arms over her chest. The nightly breeze, Dean's proximity, the recent memory of the enjoyable evening they'd spent together—all contributed to her physical reaction.

"Are you cold?" he asked, his breath tickling her skin behind her ear.

Before she had the chance to reply, he was gone and momentarily returned with a large blanket, which he draped over her shoulders.

She turned to look at him, debating with the crazy thought to step forward and ask for his arms around her. The notion quickly dispersed and she grabbed the blanket tighter, stepping away from him and the window opening. "Thanks, Dean."

He moved toward the telescope. "Let's get this situated." He pushed it forward and settled himself in front of it, looking and adjusting the small knobs. "Ah, there it is." He stepped aside and called her. "Your turn."

Sarah put her eye to it. "What am I looking at? It's all dark."

"Is it?"

He took her place in front of the telescope and readjusted it, but when she looked again, she had the same result.

"I'm sorry. I must be doing something wrong," she said, her cheeks heating with embarrassment.

"Nothing to apologize for," Dean replied.

Instead of repeating what he'd done, he came up

behind her and put his arms forward, over her shoulders. "Come closer to the eyepiece now," he said in a low voice.

The awareness of him flashed through her—his warmth, his scent, the hardness of his chest against her back. Sarah stilled.

For one long minute, time stopped as all the emotions ran through her, breath caught in her chest. Dean exhaled, wordless, immovable, as if waiting for her to do something.

He motioned to the eyepiece and she approached. "I see now," she whispered.

"The big one is Sirius, the brightest star in the Canis Major constellation," he said, still in the same hushed tone. "Orion's Belt points at it. Do you see the three stars in a line?"

She nodded, paying less attention to the stars and more to the man telling her about them. How could she not, wondering how it would feel to fully step into his arms?

The anticipation grew inside her and it was all she could think about.

Sarah turned ever so slightly and found Dean watching her, already aimed in her direction. In the low light, her other senses took over, the awareness of him heightened, and her feelings intensified in anticipation for him.

He touched her first—a hand on her hip.

Her palm splayed on his chest and he sucked in a breath.

The blanket slipped off her shoulders, but it didn't matter; cold was the last thing on her mind.

Heat flared between them and all she wanted was to get closer.

Dean's other hand came around the back of her neck and she reached up to hang on to his shoulder, searching for his mouth in the dark.

His lips found hers first—a light touch, barely a caress, a foretaste of more to come.

Not enough. Not enough.

They both returned to the other and the connection between them became firmer, stronger, deeper.

As Sarah let go of every other distraction and gave herself to kissing Dean's mouth, an explosion of sensations became everything there was—the roughness of his beard, the muskiness of his scent, the softness of his lips.

Her heart jumped, beating a new rhythm, and her breathing trembled.

Dean pulled back to inhale and she clung to him, falling against his chest. Immediately, his arms came around her and there they stayed, together, enveloped in each other, with the beat of his heart under her ear.

"Come on," Dean said after a moment. "Let's go downstairs where it's warmer."

A nod was all she had left in her after everything that had just happened.

After closing the skylight window, he took her hand and led the way to the main floor, dimming the lights as he went. And when they reached the sofa in front of the fireplace, there they fell together, and, by the light of the burning logs, they kissed again.

Again and again and again.

For a while, they didn't talk. Words might break the magic and Sarah didn't want to think, only to feel.

Later, still next to each other on the sofa, Dean played with her fingers as he held on to her hand.

"Are you okay with this? With us?" His low voice reflected some of that insecurity she'd heard in him earlier in the evening, the old shyness of the younger Dean she'd known a little before.

She touched his face and held his gaze. "I'm very okay with us."

"But?" he probed.

"How do you know there's one?"

He raised his thumb and stroked the skin at her temple. "I can see something lurking in the corner."

Sarah inhaled and released it slowly. "What happens after I leave?"

"Let's not think about that." He nuzzled the side of her neck and kissed the spot behind her ear, provoking a torrent of goose flesh. She melted, defenseless.

At her silence, he searched her eyes. "Can we think only about the now? Please?"

She agreed, of course. She would have agreed to anything Dean said, drunk on his kisses and under the spell of the amazing connection between them.

Afterward, Dean walked her home, one hand firmly clasping hers and the other holding a lantern to light the way to Conway Cabin. Charlie came along, happily strolling beside them.

She unlocked the front door and Dean stood on the threshold with her, the reluctance to part prompting their lips to meet, their arms to come around each other one last time.

"Good night, Sarah," he said at last, stepping away from her.

"Good night." She waved at him, then touched her lips, still tingling from all his kisses, and watched him and Charlie through the window.

When her phone rang, Sarah startled at the interruption. "Hello?" she answered, her voice more breathless than she intended.

"Hi, Sarah," Rachel greeted. "Peter said it's too late to call, but I told him you'd still be awake."

"Not too late. I'm awake," Sarah said.

"You're rhyming too. And you sound winded. What's going on? Is Dean there with you?"

Sarah let out a nervous chuckle. "No, Dean's not here." How typical of Rachel to pick up on something, even on the phone. "I just came home from having dinner with him and your call surprised me, that's all."

"Hold that thought," Rachel said. "I want more details on that dinner, but Peter has a question for you."

Sarah had sent Rachel and Peter an email asking him to get a specific book from her apartment, to which they had a spare key in case of an emergency. Peter came on the line and she explained to him which shelf to find the book she needed and where to mail it.

"Would you please overnight to me?" she asked.

A few sounds ensued and then Rachel replied instead of Peter. "He says he will. Now tell me more about this dinner with Dean. Where did you go? What did you eat?"

"Calm down. It wasn't that exciting." It had been completely exciting.

"Sarah, I spend my days between the couch and the bed," Rachel said. "Plus, we both know you haven't had dinner with a guy in months, if not years. Of course it's exciting."

"Has it really been years since I went out with a guy?"

"Stop stalling," Rachel said.

"Okay, okay." Sarah tried to placate her friend. "We had dinner in his home and he cooked the clams he picked on the beach yesterday."

Sarah and Rachel talked for another ten minutes. She told her friend about dessert, and Dean's telescope in the attic, and the walk home.

"I think you're holding details back from me, but I'm going to let it pass for now," Rachel said.

Sarah didn't reply. Her relationship with Dean was too new, too precious, to analyze, even with her best friend.

"Your silence is confirmation enough," Rachel continued. "As long as you understand I won't be so lenient when we meet in person."

"Who knows what will happen between now and then?" Sarah asked, as much to Rachel as to herself.

After hanging up, Sarah went through the motions of getting ready for bed, but memories of her recent time with Dean reeled in her mind.

How was she ever going to sleep?

CHAPTER EIGHT

$\mathcal{D}$ean woke up with a smile in the morning.

He'd been dreaming of kissing Sarah and she'd been kissing him back. Not as good as having the real Sarah with him, but a nice start to his day.

After seeing Sarah to her cabin last night, he'd lain awake in bed reliving all their moments together, the touches between them, the kisses that weren't enough. Just thinking about her brought the desire back in full force.

Despite the state of his heart when he fell asleep, he'd slept better than he could remember in a long time.

Having Sarah in his life was good for him, but the realization didn't surprise him. Deep down, he'd known it would be this way between them.

Violent rain against the glass panes brought him to the present.

Dean got up and approached his window to see an epic storm raging outside, too wild to discern anything beyond a few feet.

How was Sarah fairing?

He found his phone and dialed her number but it immediately went to voice mail. She might be without phone service and power.

After dressing and donning his rain slicker, he picked up his winter coat for Sarah, the one with a deep hood. Charlie followed him but when Dean opened the front door to the downpour outside, the dog went back to the rug in front of the fireplace. Smart dog.

In the incessant rain and low visibility, the short trip in his truck took a few extra minutes and, by the time he knocked on Sarah's door, he was wet despite trying to cover himself.

She answered right away. "Dean, what are you doing out in this weather?"

He stepped inside and she closed the door. "I came to check on you. I tried calling but it didn't go through." The small cabin was dark and cold. "Is the power out?"

She crossed her arms and hunched inside a large sweater. "The power is out. I think it must have gone out after I went to bed because the phone didn't charge. It's completely dead. I didn't turn the fireplace on yet. Maybe you could help with that?" she added in a hopeful tone.

"I can turn the fireplace on or you can come spend the storm at my house," he offered, hoping she would accept. "The electricity is on, the house is warm, and I'll cook you breakfast."

Her posture relaxed. "Oh, that sounds so much better. Thank you." Then she bit her bottom lip. "If you're sure I won't be in the way of you working."

"You'll absolutely not be in the way."

She slipped her phone and charger into her pocket. "Let me put on the rain boots and find my coat."

Dean undid the front of his slicker and produced his coat. "Here, take this one. It'll protect you better from the rain."

"You always think of everything," she said, with a softened expression.

The urge to embrace her was high but he saved it for later.

Within a few minutes, they were safely ensconced in his house. Dean hung their coats to dry in the utility room and brought towels for their faces and hair as they moved closer to the fireplace. Next, he brought the fire back from the coals he'd banked the night before, and replaced the screen to the front.

"How did you not lose power?" she asked.

"I have a standby generator."

"That's good." She draped the towel on the back of a chair and they stood in silence for a moment.

"Before anything else, I have an important question." Dean paused, trying to gauge her reaction, but she only looked at him, waiting.

"Yes?"

He stepped into her space and, when she didn't back away, he brought his arms around her and pulled her closer. "May I kiss you?"

A little smile pulled the corner of her mouth. "Yes, please."

She went up on tiptoes and he captured her lips, taking his time savoring a lingering kiss that only left him wanting more.

"I missed you," he confessed, his arms still holding on to her.

"I missed you too."

"Are we still okay then?"

She framed his face in her hands and kissed him squarely. "We are okay."

Breakfast was a simple affair. He cooked bacon while Sarah chopped whatever vegetables she found in the refrigerator to make omelets. Then, she toasted and buttered the leftover baguette slices, made a cup of tea for her and brewed a second pot of coffee under his supervision, since she'd managed to burn the first one while he was too distracted with her being there.

This was the kind of domestic intimacy he craved and the yearning stung his heart.

Sarah caught him rubbing his chest. "Do you have heartburn? Is it the peppers?"

Her misinterpretation made him chuckle. "No, I'm fine." It wasn't the peppers that burned his heart. "I'm just glad you're here."

Her cheeks colored slightly. "I am too. It would have been a cold day at the cabin."

That wasn't what he meant and he was sure she knew that, but he didn't correct her. In time, he'd tell her how he truly felt, and he wouldn't hold back.

She looked outside. "How long do you think the storm will last?"

"Most likely all day and maybe into the night as well." Sometimes in the fall, the storms lasted longer.

"Do you mind if I poke around your shelves to find something to read?"

"Of course not. Poke to your heart's content." He moved to his desk.

She started at the opposite end of the room and soon had a stack of books sitting on the window seat. "Don't worry," she said with a look over her shoulder, pulling out one book from the shelf. "I'll put them all back in their original spots."

"I'm not worried," he assured her. Having a librarian reorganize his bookshelves was a risk he was willing to take for the pleasure of seeing her in his home.

An hour and a half later, Sarah was still reading and Dean had finally replied to all the emails he'd neglected recently.

She stood and stretched, then crossed the room to the kitchen. "I need a break and some tea."

He came around his desk and met her. "What about some chocolate chip cookies?"

"Those would go perfect with a cup of tea." She filled the kettle and put it on the stove. "What kind do you have?"

"The kind we bake from scratch." He retrieved the recipe book from a shelf in the kitchen and opened it to the right page. "Will you read the list of ingredients while I look in the pantry?"

Sarah picked up the book and followed him. "Flour, brown sugar, white sugar, baking soda, baking powder—"

He turned around to pin a look on her. "You're reading the recipe out of order."

"Maybe. Eggs, butter—"

"Those will be in the fridge," he said, as he continued to place the various bags of ingredients on the counter in the island.

"Chocolate chips, vanilla extract, and chopped walnuts. That's it," she finished.

"I don't remember walnuts in the recipe."

"I like walnuts in my chocolate chip cookies. Do you have any?"

He went back to look and returned with a bag a quarter full, holding it up like a prize. "Whole walnuts we can chop."

"My hero." Sarah grabbed the bag and he dropped his hands to her waist, ready to claim his reward in the form of a kiss that was much too quick for his liking.

"You keep surprising me, Dean Jensen," she said, her blue eyes laughing.

A niggle of worry sprang up. "Is that good?"

"Yes, it's good. It makes me wonder what other secrets of yours I have yet to uncover."

An alarm bell rang in his head. He did have a secret he was keeping from her.

Tonight. He would tell her tonight.

After three warm-from-the-oven cookies a piece, drowsiness moved in for both of them. They exchanged yawns a few times before Dean suggested a midday nap.

It turned out that the sofa where he'd fallen asleep so many times was wide enough for two. Sarah laid in the crook of his arm and he played with her fingers with his free hand. Outside, the torrential rain continued as the day further darkened into evening.

Inside, with the warmth from the fireplace, and after a late lunch, the ambiance was decidedly languorous, and Dean's mood matched.

"I used to close my eyes and dream of all this, but now I can keep them open and see that the reality is a thousand times better."

Sarah leaned against his chest, with a lazy smile in her voice. "What was the dream?"

"This," he admitted. "You, me, and nothing else."

He felt her stiffen, then she rose to look at him. "You used to dream of us together? Is that what you mean?"

Dean sat up. "I hadn't planned to tell you like this, but I guess I'll confess I had the biggest crush on you way back then, Sarah Linden-Price."

Her mouth slacked.

He might as well tell her the rest. "Why do you think I was always the first to arrive to class? I know people teased me about it, but I didn't care that much for Ethics. It was the only way I could think of to sit by you, or rather, to have you sit by me by saving a seat in the back."

"Because I was always late coming from integrative biology on the other side of campus."

He nodded. "I took notice of that in the first few weeks."

"You never said anything."

"I was young and pathetic and lacked the confidence. I came close to asking you out so many times—so many. But at the last minute, I never had the courage to go through with it."

She took his hand. "Just so you know, I would have gone out with you."

He scooted closer to her and tightened his hold on her fingers. "You would have?"

"Of course," she hurried on to reply. "You had the kindest brown eyes—still do—and I didn't think you were pathetic. Just shy."

A smile pulled at the corners of his mouth. "I knew I was missing out, but never imagined it would be like this."

"Like what?"

Dean put his arms around her and drew her closer, inhaling the scent in her hair. "Heaven. Just heaven."

Her eyes turned serious but the moment quickly passed and she gave him a teasing smile. "You keep saying things like that, and you'll never get rid of me."

"Promise?"

She didn't reply for a moment, and he continued. "You're special to me, Sarah," he said in a low voice. "Am I crazy to think I'm not the only one feeling this connection between us?"

"You're not crazy," Sarah replied in the same hushed tone.

She leaned forward for a kiss and he met her halfway. Her lips, her taste. Her curves against his body. It was more than heaven, more than perfection, more than he had ever dreamed would be possible.

He would never tire of this, of her.

How could he, when he loved her this much already?

CHAPTER NINE

$\mathcal{S}$arah had fallen asleep on Dean's sofa and there she woke, with a blanket draped over her.

The fire burned low in the hearth and only the lights under the cupboards were on in the kitchen. A colorless light filtered through the curtains hung in front of the panoramic window, but the sounds of the rain were absent.

She rose and drew the heavy curtains open to find the view obscured by a deep, misty fog. At least the harsh rain of yesterday was gone.

"Good morning," Dean said as he came in the living room with Charlie padding after him.

He was already dressed in jeans, a T-shirt and a flannel plaid shirt over it. His hair was a little wet and combed, and he had no right to look so good in the early morning.

Dean let the dog out then came to her and hugged her from behind, wound his arms around her middle, and kissed her on the cheek.

A delicious shiver ran through her and she covered his hands with her own, a contented sigh escaping her lips.

She could get used to this so easily—to having this man in her life, waking up to his embraces, and spending her days with him.

"Did you sleep well?"

She turned sideways and brushed a kiss on his lips. "I did. Thank you for letting me crash on your sofa."

"You might have been more comfortable in the guest bedroom upstairs."

"But sleeping here among the books was much more fun. Thanks for humoring me."

"You're welcome."

Charlie barked outside and Dean hurried on to let him in, then walked to the kitchen. "Tea? Coffee? Breakfast?"

She approached the kitchen island. "Tea and breakfast sound great but I need to shower and make myself presentable." Her hair must be a complete mess. "I'm sure I look like a fright."

Dean spooned coffee grounds on the filter. "You look like your usual gorgeous self."

"I still need a shower."

"The guest bedroom upstairs has everything you need."

"Except a change of clothes and my hair brush. Plus, I need to see if the power is back on at the cabin and make sure there wasn't any damage."

"I went out early this morning to look around the cabin and my house, and only found some debris, which I cleared. But it's a good idea to check inside. I'll come with you."

Once at Conway Cabin, Sarah was relieved to not find anything broken. The power was restored and Dean lighted the gas fireplace on low.

"See you in an hour?" Dean asked on his way out.

"I might not need a whole hour. I'll be there as soon as I'm done."

"Send me a message and I'll come to walk back with you." He draped his arm around her shoulders and leaned in to kiss her on the forehead before walking out.

She stood for a moment, then touched the spot where his lips had brushed her skin. How could something so simple have so much meaning?

And when had she fallen in love with Dean?

He was right in what he'd said last night—as crazy as it sounded, the connection between them had gone from friendship to something deeper effortlessly, if a little fast.

Her departure was in two days, on Saturday morning. The taxi was scheduled to pick her up just before her rental expired, and on Monday she would be back at work at the Masterson Library in Manhattan.

Dean would continue on with his life in St. Martin's Cove, his walks on the beach with Charlie, and more time indoors in his amazing library as winter approached.

Would he miss her? Keep in touch? Did he want something more like she did or would he be content with a long distance relationship?

It didn't feel like enough, none of it.

The few times she'd brought up the subject, he'd quickly dismissed it, but maybe it was time to gently insist on an honest conversation between them.

Her phone rang and Rachel's name appeared on the screen. "Hi, Rachel," she greeted.

"Sarah, what happened yesterday? I couldn't reach you."

"There was a storm and the power went out and my phone didn't charge." It had charged later at Dean's, but Sarah hadn't even thought of calling her friend.

"Did it get very cold? What did you do to keep warm?"

"Dean invited me over. His house has a standby generator."

"That's convenient," Rachel said.

"Much better than spending the day in a cold dark cabin, but at least now everything's back to normal here."

"Are you still leaving on Saturday?" Rachel asked.

"Yes, of course. I can't wait to show you all the pictures I took."

"As excited I am to see those, it's the finished book I'm really looking forward to."

"I have some ideas to run by you when I come over," Sarah said.

"I'll make sure to send Peter out on an errand so he's not around when we discuss that. Speaking of having men around. What about you and Dean? You two have spent some time together."

A lot of time together. "Maybe some."

"What will happen when you leave?"

"I don't know honestly. We'll be talking tonight." She hoped. "I'm happy when I'm with him, Rachel."

"Then go for it, girl."

"Am I crazy to even think Dean and I have a chance?"

"You're not crazy and you won't know unless you try," Rachel said.

That thought remained with Sarah—she wouldn't know unless she tried.

What about Dean? Would he be willing to try as well?

Forty minutes later, Sarah left the cabin, locked the door, and closed the little gate behind her. The fog had dissipated some and a pale sun tried to push through. Maybe it would be sunny enough tomorrow for one last walk on the beach.

One more day with Dean.

Instead of texting him like he'd asked, she would surprise him with her early arrival and help him cook breakfast.

As she approached Dean's front door, she turned at the sound of a vehicle. The mailman exited and handed her a stack of letters and she thanked him.

She knocked and waited, then glanced down at the envelopes in her hands, but didn't find any handwritten letters.

At the back of the stack, a logo caught her eye and she stilled.

The envelope read *To Mr. Michael D. Williams, care of Mr. Michael Dean Jensen*.

Sarah stared at the words, then her eyes moved to the sender's address and the half sunburst over the ocean, the logo for Sunrise Press, based in New York.

Dean opened the door and smiled wide. "I thought I heard some knocking. Why didn't you just come in?" He kissed her cheek and pulled her inside by the hand. "The mail. Thanks for getting that," he added, taking the envelopes from her.

He called her to the kitchen and continued talking about what they should do for the day as he gathered ingredients to make breakfast.

She followed slowly. "Your first name is not Dean," she said at last.

That stopped him at what he was doing and he looked at her with a frown on his face. "What?" His eyes fell on the mail where he'd left it on the kitchen counter and he reached for it, flipping through the letters until he got to the last one.

His shoulders slumped and he looked down, easily confirming what she'd surmised.

"You're Michael D. Williams, the author of Symbols & Secrets."

"I was going to tell you, Sarah."

"Michael Dean. Is Jensen your last name?"

He nodded. "Yes. Williams is my mother's maiden name. I was named Michael after my dad and my parents called me Dean to avoid confusion."

"The D for Dean, of course," Sarah said.

"After my grandad. It's not that I didn't want you to know." He stepped towards her. "I just wanted the chance to spend time with you, be friends with you, without my pen name hovering between us. After what happened with Lisa, I didn't want you to treat me differently when you found out."

She crossed her arms. "You feared I would do the same."

"I hoped you wouldn't," he admitted. "I just wanted you to get to know me a little better before I told you."

It made sense, what with his old insecurities and shyness, but it still stung that he hadn't told her at the first opportunity.

"Why didn't you trust me?" She gestured to the book shelves. "I stood over there with your books in my hands, talked about your characters with you, and you didn't say a thing."

She turned away from Dean as she remembered what she'd said to him about author divas, the mortification washing over her. "And the comments I made. Gosh, what you must have thought of me."

"I've only thought the best of you—I think the best of you, Sarah. This is my fault." He ran a hand through his hair. "I promise I was going to tell you. I was going to tell you soon, before you left."

Hurt and embarrassment filled her chest, uncertainty and doubt taking more and more space in her mind and heart.

What did this mean for them after her departure? Had he even thought about it beyond her time in St. Martin's?

As much as she'd planned to have an honest conversation with Dean before, to ask him directly where they stood now, she couldn't anymore—not when she wasn't sure of his feelings and his trust in her. The humiliation would be too great to discover he didn't feel the same for her as she did for him. She couldn't go through this.

There would be no trying.

Somehow, Sarah pulled herself together. She had breakfast with Dean and played with Charlie and told herself her heart wasn't broken. They tried to go on as before, but a thin layer of awkwardness tinged their interactions and words, and she cringed at this new reality between them.

After a mostly-silent walk on the beach, they had a light lunch. As she thought of an excuse to return to the cabin, Dean's phone rang.

He glanced at it but didn't move to pick it up.

"You can answer," she said.

He lifted it to see the screen. "It's my agent. I'm sorry, I have to take this."

"Go ahead." She stood and walked to the front door, grateful for the opportunity to leave.

"Louis, hang on," she heard Dean say behind her. "Sarah, you don't have to go."

"I still have to clean and pack." She reminded him.

He hesitated, then said, "Are we still on for tomorrow?"

She managed a smile. "Yes, of course."

He returned to his call and she closed the door quietly, then walked to Conway Cabin.

Tomorrow was her last day and she knew Dean had something planned even though he hadn't told her what. Already she missed him. He'd become such an integral part of her life since her arrival, she could hardly fathom going back to Manhattan and resuming her normal routine without seeing him daily.

Spending this time with him would be hard, but maybe something good could come out of it—a way to say goodbye and part as friends, if nothing more. She could take the memories and be grateful for those.

When she arrived at the cabin, a small package sat on the threshold—the book she'd asked Peter to mail, her gift for Dean.

The next morning dawned brighter and warmer than the day before, even if colder than it had been prior to the storm.

Sarah was ready and waiting for Dean when a knock sounded at the door. She opened it to find him there, with Charlie beside him.

"Good morning," she said. "Let me get my coat and we can go."

She grabbed the book from the kitchen counter to give to him later.

"Sarah," Dean said.

Something about his tone and expression made her stop. "Is something the matter?"

"I came to say goodbye."

"What do you mean? Where are you going?"

"To Boston. I'm leaving in a few minutes." He let out a deep sigh. "I'm so sorry to cancel on your last day here. I had all these plans—"

"It's okay, Dean. You don't need to apologize."

"It's my agent. He's in Boston for a couple of days and asked me to come down for some meetings with him and the publisher."

Sarah nodded.

"A dinner today and a brunch tomorrow," he continued. "I won't be able to leave until after that."

"I'll be gone by then," she said. "The taxi is coming at seven thirty."

"I figured you'd be leaving early." After a pause, he added, "I wish I didn't have to go."

"It's your agent. Of course you must go."

"I haven't met with him in a while and told him I would next time he came to Boston."

"It's fine, Dean. I understand." She held out the book to him. "I have something for you. Sorry it's not wrapped."

"I didn't get you anything," he said.

"You gave me so much already, Dean. You drove me around, showed me new places, fed me excellent food. I couldn't even make you a pot of coffee without burning it."

They both chuckled lightly at the memory.

He took the book and turned it in his hands, looking over at the spine and the front page. *"The Art of Kissing in the Rain: Musings for Friday Nights at Home,"* he read. "It's the companion book to the other one I have."

"I wanted you to have both. They go together." Some things should not be kept apart.

"Where did you find it?"

"It was my copy," she told him. "I had Rachel's husband overnight it."

"I thought these were your favorites."

She shrugged. "I can only give you books. It's all I know."

"You don't need to explain," he said. "Books are your greatest treasures."

For a moment, she thought he would protest her offer, but he didn't. He understood.

"Thank you, Sarah. It'll go on the shelf next to its companion after I read it."

Before it became more awkward between them, she called Charlie over, who was only too happy to oblige.

Sarah knelt and wrapped her arms around the dog's neck. "You're a good boy, Charlie." She gave him a good rub and he wagged his tail in reply.

She stood and Dean moved forward quickly, pulling her in for a side hug and kissing the side of her head. "Take care, Sarah."

It wasn't the kind of hug she wanted, so brief she hardly touched him. "You too. Drive safely."

Sarah followed him and Charlie to the threshold as they walked back to the truck. Once inside, Dean looked her way and held out his hand, then drove away, taking her heart with him.

CHAPTER TEN

ONE WEEK LATER

$\mathcal{D}$ean stood on the sidewalk across the street from the Masterson Library in Manhattan, New York.

Sarah's shift would end in a few minutes, if he remembered correctly. In case he missed her, Michael D. Williams would call the library director and finagle Sarah's schedule under some excuse, but that was the contingency plan. Waiting for her to pass by was less stalkerish and probably more legal and moral than lying to a civil servant, however good his motives were.

The first few days after she left had been rough. Once back home from Boston and his meetings with his agent and publisher, Dean's heart ached for Sarah. He knew he would miss her but it surprised him how much and how deeply. Her eyes, her smile, the feel of her hand in his—every little thing about her and every single moment of their time together haunted him.

He hadn't heard from her but, to be fair and honest, he hadn't tried to contact her either—he'd only thought about it every day, almost every hour. After wallowing all week, picking up the phone to call her or send a message and not doing it—several times—writing emails and deleting them, he'd finally come to his senses last night. He slept for a few hours, then packed the truck with some essentials and left with Charlie in the passenger seat very early in the morning. And here he was, a week and a day after he'd last seen Sarah, hoping she wouldn't turn him away.

But Sarah was late.

He glanced at the phone screen one more time to confirm what he already knew—she was forty minutes late. Was it a normal occurrence, going home later? Was it only today? Had she used another door to go out? He could remember her saying she worked until two in the afternoon on Saturdays. Or did he have the time wrong?

This was what he got for wanting to surprise her. If he'd called her instead, and asked to meet her after work, he wouldn't still be waiting and wondering—

The phone rang in his hand and Dean almost dropped it, focused as he was on watching for Sarah to come out of the library.

The caller ID showed her name. She was calling him?

It took him another second to react and accept the call. "Sarah?"

"Dean. Hi."

It was her. He closed his eyes in relief. "Sarah, where are you?"

"Where are you?" she asked at the same time.

"I'm waiting for you to leave work." He waited for her reply, but there was only silence. "You work until two, right?"

"I usually do," she said after a pause. "Are you really in Manhattan?"

"Yes, right across the street from the Masterson Library. Waiting for you," he repeated.

"Dean, I'm not at work today. I asked for the day off."

The anticipation he'd been feeling all day deflated. "I should have called you," he said. "I wanted to surprise you and didn't even think you might not work today—"

"I did the same," she interrupted.

Now he was confused. "What do you mean?"

"I wanted to surprise you too and didn't call to check."

"Where are you?" He asked her, hope rising again.

"I'm in St. Martin's Cove, outside your front door. I thought you'd be here—"

"You wanted to surprise me," he added. "How did you even manage to get there so early in the afternoon?"

"It's a long story and a longer trip," she replied with a smile in her voice. "What do we do now?"

He heard the fatigue as well. It had taken him almost nine hours to drive to Manhattan but her travels had surely taken longer using public transportation.

"Sarah, I have a spare key hidden by the back door. Let me tell you exactly where it is." He gave her instructions on where to locate the emergency key and waited until she was safely inside, then told her how to turn off the house alarm, turn it back on, and switch on the central heating instead of lighting a fire. "There are ready-to-eat meals in the freezer and soup mixes in the pantry. Will you—will you wait for me?"

"I'm not going anywhere. Just promise me you'll drive safely and be careful," she asked. "I'll wait for you."

It was late by the time he arrived in St. Martin's Cove. He kept his promise and drove safely, stopping as needed for him and Charlie, and it was well past midnight when he parked the truck in the driveway.

Sarah had left all the flood lights on, as if to light the way for him, to welcome him back. He found her on the sofa, sleeping soundly, and his heart leapt at the sight. Charlie plopped himself on the rug, content to be near her, and Dean went to his bedroom, where he fell in bed with a smile on his lips.

He woke with a start the next morning.

Sarah and Charlie were gone and Dean found

a sticky note on the kitchen counter—*Walking with Charlie*—which explained their absence.

The morning was half gone and he could hardly wait to see Sarah again. He got a quick shower, and when he returned to the family room, Sarah had just come back with Charlie.

They didn't move at first, only watched each other for a moment.

"You're up," she said, then closed the door and removed her coat.

Dean grinned. "You're here."

"I told you I'd wait."

He nodded, still smiling. "You did say that."

Slowly, Dean made his way around the room, waiting for a cue from her.

Sarah watched him with some hesitation. "I didn't think you'd go to Manhattan."

"I have an apartment in the West Village. I can move there for the winter, if I need to. That's where I left Charlie when I was waiting at the library."

She grabbed a nearby chair and sat on it. "But you said—I remember you said you'd only move to the city for a very strong reason."

He held her gaze. "I have a very strong reason to move to the city, Sarah."

"But the peace and quiet," she continued. "For your work?"

He pulled out the nearest chair to hers and sat facing her, only a few feet away. "I'm a writer. I can write from anywhere."

"It might be harder to keep your pen name a secret there," she argued weakly.

"Maybe it's time Michael D. Williams reveals his identity."

"You're really going to do all this?" she asked in a low voice.

Dean leaned forward, his eyes never leaving hers. "For a chance with you—for you—I'll do whatever it takes."

Sarah squeezed her eyes shut and covered her mouth with her fingers, turning away from him.

He held his breath, waiting for a word from her.

Had he said too much too soon?

"I lied when I asked you to think only about the now. I want everything, Sarah, everything we can fit in between now and forever. If you think we're worth the—"

In a swift movement, she left the chair and sat sideways on his lap, wrapping her arms with surprising force around his neck.

Dean pulled her against him and buried his face in her hair, the familiar sweet scent filling his senses. He closed his eyes and sighed.

"I couldn't stop thinking of you." Her tone was urgent. "I've missed you so much."

"My heart ached for you every day," he confessed. "Why did you come, Sarah?"

She tipped her chin toward the coffee table where a square box sat. "I made a photo book for you of all the places we went together. It's too precious to put in the mail."

"Thank goodness for that," he admitted.

She pulled back a little and searched his eyes. "Are you really willing to move to Manhattan?"

He nodded. "You'll never get rid of me."

"Promise?"

"That's a promise I'll keep, because I love you, Sarah."

"And I love you," she said.

He framed her face with his hands and brought his lips to hers, saying more with the kiss than words could ever express.

As long as he had her in his arms, he had everything.

EPILOGUE

$\mathscr{S}$arah and Dean, and Charlie had come to the beach house for the weekend.

With the federal holiday on Monday, Sarah didn't have to work that day. She'd asked for Saturday off and they'd left the city before the sun was up. Almost three whole days at their favorite place.

When they arrived at St. Martin's Cove, the weather was clear and sunny, although cold, and the three of them bounded to the beach before doing anything else. It had been a while and they'd missed it fiercely.

Dean and Charlie went on ahead, tossing a ball back and forth until the dog's attention veered somewhere else, then Dean walked back to her, put this arm around her shoulders, and kissed her on the forehead.

"What do you want to do after dinner?" he asked.

"Read by the fire and cuddle." She snuggled up to him in anticipation.

"Are you cold?" he asked her. "Do you want to go back now?"

"We can stay for a little longer before it gets too dark." The days were still too short and cold to enjoy the evening outside. "I can't wait for summer. It'll be so nice to go in the water and stay out here till late."

"Each season has something I like," Dean said, "something to look forward to." His expression turned pensive.

"Do you miss living here year-round?" Sometimes doubts sneaked in.

"No," he replied without hesitation. "I like it here, but it's just a house and a place. As long as we're together, we can live anywhere you want."

"You're right." Sarah nodded and held on to his arm closer. "I feel the same."

Dean stopped and put his hands on her shoulders, then dropped a quick kiss on her mouth. "Stay here. Don't move."

He whistled and called for Charlie. "Here, boy. Come here, Charlie."

Charlie trotted toward them, but when he saw Dean approaching, the dog started zooming around. The more Dean called after him, the more Charlie ran.

Sarah chuckled. "What's going on? What are you two doing?

"Stay there, Sarah. We're coming." Dean called his dog again, but Charlie wouldn't come, playing his version of a game of tag.

After another minute of chasing after Charlie, Dean threw his hands in the air and jogged back to her.

"The one time I need his help and he thinks it's a game." He shook his head lightly with a smile on his face.

"What do you need his help for?"

Dean came to a spot in front of her, the tips of their boots touching, slipped his hand in his coat pocket and drew out a small box. "With this."

It took her second to realize what he meant, then she gasped and covered her mouth with her hands.

He looked around for a quick moment then nodded to himself. "This is about the spot where we met again last October, and I had this grand idea and planned everything in my mind where Charlie would help carry the box to you and—" He paused and took a breath. "I'm rambling."

He inhaled again then fumbled with the box and took out the ring and gazed at her. "Sarah, you know I love you. With all my heart. I can't live the rest of my life without you in it every day. Will you marry me?"

She couldn't look away from him. She opened her mouth to reply, but her voice faltered and she cleared her throat. "Yes. Yes," she repeated more clearly.

Her heart beat too fast and her hand trembled as she extended it to Dean. He took it firmly in his and slipped a ring onto her finger, his smile growing wider.

When his arms came around her tightly, Sarah went on her tiptoes and laced her hands behind his neck. Their lips met, sweetly at first, then more deeply, sealing their commitment to each other.

After a moment, Dean smiled again, twirled her around and whooped. "You said yes."

"Of course I said yes." Sarah wiped the tears that had escaped her eyes and chuckled. "Did you think I wouldn't?"

He embraced her again, touching his forehead to hers. "I didn't want to presume."

"You didn't have to presume," she replied. "You know I love you too, and this is what I want as well, our lives together."

Charlie bumped Dean's leg and he faltered, then recovered his balance. "You missed your chance, Charlie. It's my turn."

Sarah laughed, as full of happiness as she'd ever felt before.

"Come on," Dean said, draping an arm over her shoulders. "Let's go home and celebrate."

Home. Together.

RECIPES

Steamed Clams

4 pounds clams soaked, scrubbed, rinsed and cleaned
1 tablespoon butter
1 tablespoon olive oil
3 cloves garlic, finely chopped
½ cup finely, chopped onion or shallot
¼ cup white wine
3 tablespoons finely chopped fresh chives and parsley
2 lemons, one for juice and zest, and 1 cut in wedges for serving
Grilled baguette for serving

In a large skillet, heat the butter and olive oil. Add the garlic and chopped onion, and cook until garlic is fragrant. Add the wine and clams and increase the heat. Cover the skillet and cook until the clams have opened. Time varies with the size of the clams. When the clams are cooked, remove the ones that did not open. Add the chopped fresh herbs and the juice from one lemon. Stir.

To serve, spoon into four bowls or soup plates. Garnish with lemon wedges and pieces of grilled baguette to sop up the broth.

Roasted blueberries in yogurt-cheese mousse

    1 1/2 cups heavy cream, cold
    1/4 cup granulated sugar
    3 ounces cream cheese at room temperature
    2 ounces of plain yogurt, at room temperature
    2-3 cups blueberries

Preheat the oven to 400 degrees F and line a baking sheet with aluminum foil. Place the cream cheese and the yogurt in a large bowl and set aside.

In a large stand mixer with the whisk attachment, beat the heavy cream and sugar to a stiff peak (this can also be done by hand.)

Spoon half of the whipped cream into the bowl with the cream cheese and plain yogurt, and whisk vigorously until smooth. Add the remaining whipped cream and gently fold to combine. Cover and chill in the refrigerator.

Place the blueberries on the prepared baking sheet and roast in 4 minute intervals, shaking the pan at each interval to ensure that the berries roast evenly. They should be nice and roasted after 12-16 minutes.

Spoon the mousse into small bowls and top with the roasted blueberries.

Dear Reader,

*T*hank you so much for reading Sarah and Dean's story, *Between Now and Forever.* I hope you've enjoyed reading it as much as I enjoyed writing it.

Please consider leaving a review on Goodreads and other online book retailers. This is the best way to support me as an author.

For news of upcoming books and promotions, join my readers club.

I love to hear from readers! You can email me at lucinda@lucindawhitney.com.

Thank you!

THE AUTHOR

$\mathcal{L}$ucinda Whitney was born and raised in Portugal, where she received a Master's degree from the University of Minho in Braga, in Portuguese/English teaching.

She lives in northern Utah with her husband and four children. When she's not reading and writing, she can be found with a pair of knitting needles, or tending her herb garden.

She's the author of the *Romano Family* series, and the co-author of the *Royal Secrets* series with Lindzee Armstrong and Laura D. Bastian.

Please visit her website at lucindawhitney.com for more information and news.